LOVE AT FI[...]

A NOVEL IN VERSE

# PIZZA GUISE

VERA WEST

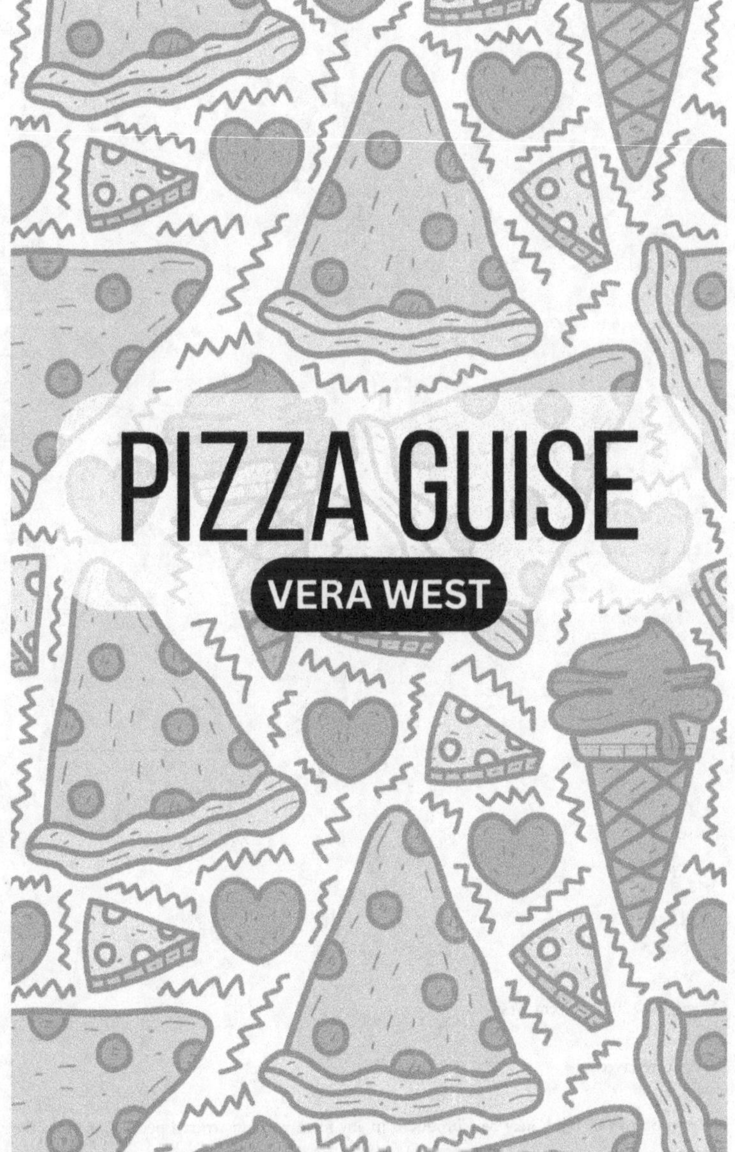

# PIZZA GUISE

VERA WEST

Copyright © 2026 by Vera West.

To my little Meatball. We'll miss you always.

To my little Meatball. We'll miss you always.

PART ONE

**1**

Leaning against the wall,
   just out of reach
   from the suds-filled sink,
   I smirked at my four brothers;
   wiped a smudge
   of flour off my thumb
   and turned the page.

"It's a universal truth," I declared grandiosely,
   "that a man with the ability to lean
   must be in want of something to clean."

"You're the one who's *leaning*,"
   Leo muttered from the non-slip mats
   as he pushed pans off
   the counter's cliff-edge
   into the sink.

"Why *aren't* you helping us?" Kit growled
   as he paused sweeping

the dingy mop-head around
the red-brick-tiled floor.

I ignored them entirely and waved
*Pride and Prejudice* in the air.
"Check this," I said, clearing my throat
to paraphrase, "our man just
proposed and his (wannabe) girl
is offended because he told her
that despite everything
her rude family,
lack of cash,
even her homey face,
couldn't stop him from loving her."

"That doesn't sound like love," Mario
interjected, carrying stacked containers
of freshly chopped pizza toppings
to the walk-in fridge.

"Miss me with that corny stuff,"
Leo snapped, "if Elijah was actually
*helping*, I'd be getting a DVD
from Brickbuster's right now."

Leo chucked his yellow
Scrub Daddy at the industrial sink;
it skipped like a nylon stone
between pans and spoons and lids
until it sunk down deep

into the dirty dishwater.

"Have fun fishing that out," I teased.

Leo groaned,
the display of
authentic angst, almost
making me feel sorry
for him, but every little turd
must grow up one day
and my youngest brother
was the most entitled one I knew.

"Man, how we own a whole Pizza Palace,
but we can't fix our dishwasher?"

"How would we own half?" Mario jabbed.

"Didn't realize you needed fixing, Leo," I jived.

Leo gritted his teeth. "Both of y'all *shut up*."

"I'd agree," interjected James
from the back office diplomatically,
"silence would help everyone's focus."

James, myself, Mario, Kit-Kat "Karl" and Leo,
all the Bennet Brothers of
the East Side Plaza,
a horseshoe shaped

outside mini mall featuring:
Bubbles (laundromat)
Brickbuster's (video rental)
Great Giant (groceries)
Petal Pushers (flowers)
Bingo Balls (my parents loved alliteration)
and one local owned pizzeria: Pizza Palace.

"Elijah is reading to us
rather than helping us," Kit snitched.

"Reading is fundamental," I said cheerily.

"Man," Leo whined, "you ain't even
reading, you're paragraphing."

"*Paraphrasing,*" Mario corrected.

"I rest my case," I teased.

"You ain't Olive Benson," Leo snapped.

Kit laughed, "Benson is the cop. You should read more."

"Law and Order is a TV show, not a book!" Leo yelled.

James let out a piercing whistle
and all eyes were on him.
"Elijah and I will finish closing up.
You three can go to Brickbuster's."

Even Mario, who would always
rather be reading
ran out as quickly as he could.
They'd successfully gotten out
of work but the real win
was the uninterrupted
share-tax free snacking
that would promptly
begin when the final chores
were completed.

**2**

— · —

MY PARENTS' ORIGIN STORY
   (Missie and Monte)
   started as high school sweethearts
   unwilling to give up
   in their hometown.

   Pizza Palace's first tenants,
   destined to buy out the
   original mini-mart owners
   when they were ready to retire;
   the McGregors,
   having no ambitious heirs,
   were honestly just happy it sold.

   The mart was run down bad
   but my parents dreamed
   of what it could become,
   the mecca it could be
   and began investing
   sweat equity
   into Great Giant,

then, slowly, determinedly,
all the other buildings too,
renovating and redesigning
until their last project, Bingo Balls,
a hall that doubled
as a community center
when we weren't hosting
weekend bingo nights.

The money was just enough
to eat good and hire locally;
*staying open* was the dream now.

That mattered most
to my mother,
her love language
being acts of service:
seeing needs
serving needs
and the mini mall was
our neighborhood's lifeline,
and any adjacent neighborhood
within walking distance.

What matters most
to my father,
was eventually retiring.
What mattered most to me,
was somewhere in the middle.

Between entrepreneurial thoughts
and my need to retrieve
a rogue bell pepper that had slid far
under the pizza-topping counter,
I didn't hear the customer approaching
until someone began rapid-fire-ringing
the counter bell for help.

**3**

"WHAT'S TAKING THEM SO long?"
"Stop ringin' the bell."
"There he is!"

Their voices mingled,
mixing together as
I headed from the back
to the front of the store.

I noticed the quiet one first;
decadent brown skin,
warm brown eyes,
soft brown hair,
that glowed under the light
with an aura that felt
like it filled the whole space.
She was dressed in a
casual-elevated way;
her oversized sweater,
a peek of legging covered thighs
just above her knee-high boots

was giving intellectual boss vibes;
she could do the job better
and tell you exactly why that was.

It was so *sexy*.

Looking at her phone,
thumb casual flicking as she scrolled,
but when she felt my stare
her eyes turned up to meet mine
and she crinkled her nose in surprise.

Surprise that I was staring
or surprise that I didn't care
she'd caught me?
I flashed her a smile
and winked;
you had to be all in
with this sort of thing, you know?
Between you and me,
I was praying the wink
was a wink and not a twitch.
She made another face at me,
as if she thought I was
a completely goofy idiot,
Over exaggeratedly winked back
and shot two laser guns in my directions.
I hadn't expected *that*
and now Miss Sunshine surely
felt mocked as I chuckled

through asking her, "How can I help you?"

"Did you just wink at my friend?"
"Maybe," I half-admitted.
"Cheeky," she said with a laugh.

If I hadn't been embarrassed before,
I was now.

"Is it too late to order?" Sunshine
asked. "We're not from around here
and heard this place has the best pizza pie."
"Actually, we just—" I began but
James interrupted me.

"Of course! Are you planning on dining in?"
*Dining in,* I scoffed internally;
James was serious,
eyes bright and focused
grinning bigger than I'd
ever seen him smile—
all of it aimed at the
young lady standing
adjacent to the counter.

"Can I have your name
for the order?"
Another thing we never did.

"Bianca Bingley," she said.

"What a pretty name," James
murmured unlike himself;
very *much* unlike himself.
His eyes filled
with hopes and hearts.

"Can you take my order then?" Bianca asked.
"You can order me, yes."
She giggled. "What?"
James flushed. "Yes, what would you like?
Bianca smiled prettily,
leaning forward murmured, "Are you on the menu?"
James froze
under her temptress gaze
and I was sure he'd
come to melt into pure goo.

"James isn't FDA approved
so sadly he isn't on the menu
but a one-topping-pizza
for nine-ninety-nine
plus tax, is," I advised.

Bianca gave me a wink
and said:
"Peperoni
onion
and bell pepper, please."

"The deal only applies

to one topping," James clarified.

"That's fine. I'll pay extra.
we'll also need three large sodas."

I patted James on the back.
"I've got it, go make
their pizza."

**4**

"Y'ALL ARE NEW TO town?"
I asked as I rang up their order.

"Yes, you see Darcy there?" Bianca said
with a point over her shoulder.

I nodded.

Darcy scoffed, frowning,
clearly disapproving of her friend's
inevitable habitual praise.

"She's brilliant," Bianca bragged,
"looking at properties to develop into–"

Bianca looked over her shoulder,
her friend stepping forward.

"Low-income housing," Darcy explained,
"community centers or charter schools;
whatever makes sense."

I raised an eyebrow
skeptically hung up on
the flippancy of her
word choice *whatever*.
We had low-income housing,
and community centers,
and charter schools;
we didn't need more,
we needed better,
we didn't need new,
we needed inclusion.

"Anything in your
development repertoire,"
I asked, "that enriches,
rather than alters?"

Darcy met me gaze for gaze.
"Like I said, we'll develop whatever
the community needs."

"Then, it'd behoove you
to actually consider what
the *community* needs;
profitability isn't king."

"That is a very good
point," Bianca surmised.

Darcy smirked wickedly,
hands placed firmly on
the counter as she leaned in.
"Can we have our over-priced sodas now?"

I found myself leaning in too,
matching her malice mouth
grin for grin.
"Sure can," I said, holding her
gaze as I reached
for the adjacent cups,
then tapping them down
in front of her with a loud *clap*.
"Lids and straws are over there,
let me know if there's not enough *fizz*."

# 5

—·—

A LITTLE WHILE LATER
the pizzas were done
and James was carefully
packing them to go.

I gave him space,
watching him approach
the counter as Bianca
hopped up immediately to
meet him at the register.

"You mentioned you were
new to town?" James asked,
his tone a quiet mellow.

Bianca nodded enthusiastically.

A pause—
brief enough, but long enough
to stir suspense.
"I could show you around—

if you want," James offered.


"I would like that very much."
Bianca beamed. "Darcy is great
but such a grump, you know?
I want to see fun places and all
she wants to do is look at
investment opportunities."


"Do you like to skate?
If you want to learn
about the area that would
be a fun start. I know a great spot;
lots of heart at that rink."


"Really? Are you good at skating?"
Bianca asked.


James leaned forward with a
suave tilt I didn't know he had in him
and said, "I'm the best."


Bianca matched his energy,
eyes gleaming
as she leaned forward too,
"Then you'll be the perfect teacher."


James nodded and slid her pizzas
towards her.

"I'm free next Thursday," Bianca said,
"that work for you?"
James ripped the receipt
from the printer,
nodding yes, as he scribbled
his number on the back.

"Give me a call
and we'll set a time."

Bianca leaned in again,
and I felt like I was watching
the cheesiest rom-com *ever*.
Taking his hand in hers,
she turned it up,
and wrote her number
across his palm.

"I think you should call me."

I could hear James gulp
from across the room
and it took a lot to stifle my chuckle.
He was just so easy to read;
pizza sauced stained heart
on his sleeve.
Bianca better be good to him.

# 6

IT TOOK MONTHS,
way longer than it should have,
for me to convince my
parents to let me move out.

Everything was a matter of
convenience to them,
family businesses,
family matters,
family living situations
their children were their binkies
and they clutched us close.
It had always been a buzz kill
and with mid-twenties approaching
for me and late twenties creeping up
on James, enough was enough.
You see,
all of the mini-mart buildings
had second story units.

Above Brick Buster

was an elderly couple,
retired general motors workers
married some thirty plus years,
above Petal Pushers
were long-term tenants
who also sold the flowers,
and above Pizza Palace
(two units reno'd into one)
was where all the Bennet boys
had grown up.

Three two-bedrooms, one bath above
Bingo Balls, Bubbles, Brickbuster's
were the only spaces still vacant;
originally because they'd needed
the most work, but now,
in the current economic climate
rapidly becoming the normal temperature,
the juice wasn't worth the squeeze.
There's nothing quite like
a midwestern wind chill, is there?
Begrudgingly, we were set free
to move above Bubbles'
(oddly fresh, thanks to the
plethora of fresh linen-scented
detergents vented up into)
two-bedroom apartment.

"I texted her last night,"
James said with a sigh

from the sofa in our living room.

It had been
six sunsets,
seven sunrises
since serendipity.
James had Bianca on the brain;
it was a good look for him,
I'd never seen him smitten like this.

Bianca's friend, Darcy,
had casually been
on my mind too.
Mainly I thought of her
whenever James mentioned
Bianca; but the thoughts
were shallow and fleeting
at best.

How many romances
should one love story tell?
I don't make the trope rules,
it's canon.

"I think she likes me,"
James prattled on, "but,
you know I'm not good at
this stuff."

"If she likes you,"

I said reassuringly,
"she'll think you're
good at all the right stuff."

"I'd feel better if you
were there too," James confessed.

I almost dared not ask, "Where?"
"Rollhaven, tomorrow night."
"Won't I be a third-wheel?" I asked.
"Not at all, Darcy will be there too,"
James assured me.
But I didn't feel very assured.

**7**



If you've never been
to a rink, it's hard to
describe the vibe,
but there's *always* a vibe.

Energy crackling
as bodies roll by,
some synchronized
others staggering on wobbly legs
but everyone's having
a good time.

Truly, I'd agree to come
to Rollhaven for two reasons:
James needed moral support
and someone needed to
watch after Kit and Leo
because (of course) once
my parents knew we were going,
they were coming too which meant
*everyone* had to go.

Mario immediately found a corner
and opened  e-reader;
I'll admit, the backlighting was handy.

My parents were already giggling
with each other like it was
1980 and they were kid-less and free.

It would have been cute
if their public displays
of affection weren't so *cringe*.

I'd have to watch them;
if any Marvin Gaye played
they'd be turning heads
with their notorious couples' skating
and Bianca would get the wrong
–which would actually be the right–
impression of our family.

Maybe it was good
for her to know sooner
whether she could
handle us or not.

James was cool,
and I was well-read at reading rooms,
but the rest of them?
Denser than fruit cake.

I was always torn between
defending and disowning
my family, but I stuck by them;
flawed as they were,
they were all I had
and I wasn't a person
who could just give up.

**8**

—·—

I scanned the rink
for Bianca and James,
finding them shoulder to shoulder
against the edge of the room;
he was bent over, helping her
tie on a rented retro pair of skates

Bianca was listening attentively
to James' explanation of why
we crisscross laces
over rather than under;
and when his hand
absentmindedly
brushed her thigh
as he sat up, I could see the
flush in her cheeks
from all the way over here.

"What are we looking at?"
a voice asked from behind me.

I turned to see
my childhood friend
(whose family owned Petal Pedal Pushers)
Charlotte "Charmander" Perkins.
Commonly shortened to Char.
James had been Squirtle.
I was obviously Bulbasaur
for my brutish strength but
loveable roguish charm.

"Charmander!" I bellowed.
Charlotte always feigned annoyance
when I called her that
but truth be told,
she loved it, or I loved it
enough to withstand any backlash.

"Who's with Squirtle?" she asked.
"Someone he hopes tames him." I answered.
"He wants her to hold him captive
in a Poke ball and force him to fight?"
"Super hot, right?" I teased.
Charlotte laughed.
"It's a blast burn, no doubt,"
"Nerd!" I exclaimed.
"But really," Charlotte pressed, "who is she?"

"Wealthy developers from out of town,
–or, at least  she is a developer–
not sure about Bianca's occupation

but she's nicer than her friend, that's for sure."

"Is that *her friend* wobbling over here?"
Charlotte casually asked.

I shifted my focus,
and sure enough,
on very shaky legs
Darcy was headed our way.

I rushed over,
convinced that if I didn't
steady her, Darcy'd fall
and bust her pretty ass;
Not that I'd noticed her ass.
"Let me give you a hand,"
I said, reaching for her,
but, of course, Darcy adamantly
waved me away, causing her arms
to flutter as she lost her balance.

Just a few inches above ground,
I caught her by the waist
nose to nose,
her eyes a pretty brown,
but her sharp tongue too quick.

"Let me go," Darcy barked
through gritted teeth.
I matched her scowl for scowl.

"Shouldn't you be thanking me?"
"Thanks, now set me down!"

A mix of angry-embarrassment,
Darcy's face reddening by the second,
her wheeled-feet slid over the carpet
as she desperately tried to right herself.

I pointed over her shoulder
to a bench not far away.
"Let's get you to that seat over there," I suggested
but she vehemently shook her head
insisting I *leave her be.*

I did something
I'm not proud
of but don't exactly regret,
I dropped her.

**9**

—·—

Pizza Palace doesn't open
   until early afternoon;
   no one comes by our joint
   for lunch, and whenever I can,
   (preferably on Thursday mornings)
   I go uptown
   to the swanky area
   where historic buildings
   have been bestowed enough love
   to draw tourists to main street.

   It's an aesthetically pleasing
   block of streets, obviously,
   because I'm there too,
   and when I do venture out of my
   hood and into the mainstream
   hustle and bustle,
   my favorite place to get lost
   is The Bitter End.

   First floor coffee shop,

second floor bookstore;

originally, as the lore goes,

The Bitter End only sold sad books

but sooner or later

everyone seductively succumbs

to the one genre that

will always keep the lights on:

romance.


Intellectual porn,

and I love it,

escapism at its finest,

and I need it;

*hope is a*

*thing with feathers*

and I want it

perched forever in my soul.


My eyes shift up from

the edge of my book

over the rim of my coffee,

distracted from an action packed romantasy

to the seemingly more and more

familiar silhouette of Darcy.


"You drink coffee too,"

I murmured, or at least,

I meant to, but I must

have said it loud enough

because she turned on a dime and

smiled.

My earth stood still;
coffee lingering
in the back of my throat,
my heart frozen
at rest until it took another beat,
meanwhile, my inner monologue
rambling on
about not only how dumb of a thing to say
but how dumb of a way to respond to a smile.

I couldn't really
be losing it
over someone
who didn't even like me,
right?
That'd be the definition of *pathetic*.

No, I was good,
everything was fine,
I just hadn't expected
that smile.
That was all.
I forced myself to still,
to take big swig of my tea,
and certainly not watch
her figure move through
the line out of the corner of my eye.

When her name was called
and she retried her drink
I exhaled, recommitting to my book,
relieved our interaction was done,
but then I felt the energy shift
and knew without needing to look
that Darcy was about to join me
at my table.

# 10

_–.–_

"YOU DRINK COFFEE TOO, huh?"
I awkwardly repeated.

Darcy motioned towards my mug,
"Isn't that tea?"

I glanced at my cup,
it's *a gift to be simple*
inspirational printed quote
shining like a neon sign.

I shrugged
and Darcy smiled,
victoriously taking
her throne across from mine,
shifting my backpack
to an adjacent chair
to make room for her arms
to frame the steaming coffee
she'd carefully set down.

Hooking the handles
of her oversized leather tote
around the corners of her chair
Darcy finally seemed situated just right;
reminding me of a dachshund
spinning twenty times before laying down.

I let an intrusive thought slip,
envisioning how enraged she'd be
if I booped her snoot
and told her she was a good girl.
Well, she might like one of
of those two things–

"What are you reading?" she calmly asked,
her relaxed velvet voice sultry sweet,
like Toni Braxton or Alicia Keys.

"I specifically read on an
e-reader so no one knows."

A hint of a smirk teased her cheeks.

"A romance reader! I'm surprised
that I'm not actually *surprised*."
She'd hooked me.
"Why's that?" I asked.

"You run a family business,
read in coffee shops

while drinking tea,
not to mention your
Usher level skating skills;
you're a modern renaissance man,
Elijah Bennet."

I acknowledge her
accuracy with a beguiled
*humph.*

She was teasing,
of course,
but that didn't make
her any less spot on.

"Which one?" Darcy asked.
"Which one?" I echoed.
"Which smut are you devouring?"
"Aren't you flirty by daylight," I murmured.

Darcy wasn't just flirty,
she was down right charismatic.
How could someone go from
being a grumpy little Care Bear
to a mischievous goddess of rizz?

I was not prepared for this.

"I haven't even acknowledged
that your guess was right,"

I reminded her.

She cocked her head,
arched her eyebrow,
and I folded immediately.

"Cozy modern day western,
I just finished a good romantasy
if you're taking recommendations."

Darcy folded her hands under
her chin and gave me my first
full smile.

"I am."

It was a bet,
a dare to see—what?
I wasn't sure exactly.
If I really read romances?
If she'd really read
something I'd suggested?
Even unsure, I still
choose to take the bait;
she had dimples after all.

Her eyes watched my hand
reach into my messenger bag,
digging as I fished
for the book I'd just mentioned.

I didn't keep books I hated,
I never got rid of books I loved,
so *Blood Like Rubies* had to be
buried somewhere in my bag;
her gaze was just so distracting.
Finally!
I found it and slid it across the table.

Darcy chuckled—almost too low
for me to hear, but I caught it;
the wind of her laugh,
the rich mocha infused scent
of coffee beans lingering on
her breath as it whirled around me.

I'd better take care, I thought,
her essence is too potent.

"Read a little," I said,
nodding towards the book,
"you'll know within the
first few lines if it's right for you."
"I don't know," Darcy quipped,
leaning back, settling into her chair,
posture primed for reading,
"sometimes it takes me awhile."

**11**

WE SAT THERE,
  together
  reading long past our
  drinks becoming cold,
  until she was unconsciously
  smiling while she read
  and I was peeking over my ereader
  watching her turn pages,
  studying her reactions,
  gauging where she was
  by the thickness of the read
  pages piling up.

I couldn't look away;
when a smile curved against her lips,
I knew *she knew* I'd been staring.

"Reading me rather than your book?"
Darcy asked without looking up.

"What do you think so far?" I replied.

Darcy finally look up at me
and I was captivated by the
relaxed warmth of her gaze.


"I like it more than I thought I would,"
she answered candidly.


I could only nod in response,
unsure if she meant me
or the book; perhaps both even,
two things could be true.


Darcy looked at her watch,
which made me look at mine;
it was well into the afternoon now.


She began gathering her things,
and I mimicked her,
suddenly feeling very unsettled,
(which was unironically quite unsettling)
and afraid that without something to do,
my unoccupied mind would
allow my mouth to ramble.


"Do you come here every Thursday?"
Darcy asked once packed.
I nodded yes.
"Good," she beamed, "I'll see you next week."

# 12

TRUE TO HER WORD,
     we began a cadence
     of reading over hot drinks
     every Thursday.
     I had a suspicion that
     Darcy only read with me;
     her progress always starting
     where we'd last ended.

# 13

I SMILED APPROVINGLY AT
the contents of my wok.
The huge bamboo-handled pan
was a game changer and,
—not gonna lie—
I didn't just use it for stir-fry,
I used that shit for everything.
Don't ever question
a man with a pan.

The knock was so soft
I didn't hear it
until the fourth or fifth
rap against the door.

I wasn't expecting anyone
but there an unspoken exception
that one of my other brothers
would stop by;
Mario hiding from the chaos,
Kit-Kat annoyed with Leo

or Leo annoyed with everyone,
yet, when I opened the door it was *Darcy*.

"James sent me over,"
she explained in a rush
of words as she took in
my surprised countenance.

My mind felt like a stuttering car
hopping to the next thought
before I'd finished the last;
she's here in my,
why did she,
she looks so pretty,
thank god I'm wearing pants,
is that my—

"Is that my book you're holding?"
I finally spat out.
Darcy nodded yes, offering it to me.
We stared at each other
a couple of awkward turtles,
until she sniffed the air
and we asked in unison:
*Can I come in?*
*Do you want to come in?*

I let out a nervous laugh
entangled with a sigh.

"It's decided then," I said, sheepishly,
"you're coming in."


Darcy grinned. "Apparently."


I stepped back
so she could step in,
and was dazzled by her
instant disrobing of clothes—er, jacket;
I took her coat and her purse too,
unceremoniously hanging them on
the tall kitchen-island chair.


"Are you hungry?" I asked.
"I could eat," Darcy replied,
taking a seat in the chair
I'd marked with her belongings.


"I didn't mean to barge in,"
she continued, "but I came by
Pizza Palace, and James
sent me here. He was sure
you wouldn't mind the company."


"He was right," I said, focusing on
stirring and frying, frying and stirring,
trying desperately to compose
myself into seeming less giddy.


"I finished reading your book,"

Darcy added, "and I couldn't wait to—"

"Tell me how excellent my taste is?"
I interrupted teasingly.

"I was going to stay,
*steal another,* but yes,
you do have impeccable taste."

Darcy's lips teased into a
smile I wanted to bite.
Get a hold of yourself,
my monologue chided.

"After we eat you can
*kiss* me."

"Kiss you?" I asked
"Quiz me," she repeated.
"Quiz you," I confirmed,
trying to allege in my tone
that it was a simple mistake
but it was too late, and she,
far too clever to let it slip by.
"Elijah Bennet," Darcy drawled,
coyly, "where exactly has
your mind been going when
you think about me?"

I turned away from the stove,

leaning over the island as if
it were a protective barrier
but then she bridged the gap
closing the space between us
as she leaned forward too,
and suddenly I was
face-to-face
with my sexist adversary.

It felt like all the things
I knew to be fictional
were reality:
magnetic pulls,
electric charged air,
fluttered lashes,
flush cheeks,
heated looks
and lips *damn*
her lips just had to be ki—

"Oh no," James' voice sighed
from the door, "I'm interrupting, aren't I?"

I felt the tether snap,
the moment gone,
the stir fry sizzling.

I quickly spun around,
too shy, too chicken,
to steal a glance at Darcy.

I felt a light touch on my arm,
Darcy had moved from
her island perch to
stand beside me in the kitchen.

"I should go," she murmured
and as I turned to face her
she rose up on her toes
to brush a quick kiss against
my cheek.
"Call me sometime,
take me out,
my number's in your book."

I caught her elbow
and before I could
think myself out of
what I'd been dying to
do to just moments before
I pulled her back to me
and tilted my head down
as she rose up once more
for a kiss.

# 14

Silk,
   that's how soft
   her kiss was,
   that's how light
   her touch on my arm was
   as she pulled me closer.

Decadent,
   a rich kiss that deepened
   as we bit into the indulgence
   we'd been craving nearly starving for;
   time slowed as we grew utterly
   enthralled in our moment.

James coughed
   and the spell snapped.
   "Sorry," he whispered, "old buildings are drafty."

I smirked at the absurdity of it all;
   looking down at Darcy,
   her eyes still dazed,

a blush subsiding
from her cheeks,
clearly we both felt it,
this unexpected heat
this unsettling need;
a charismatic fire
that we'd flame,
growing until it consumed us.

"Call me," Darcy murmured again,
an echo of our midwestern goodbye
that had started a lifetime ago,
and I was still nodding *yes*
even as I closed the door
softly behind her.

# 15

— · —

JAMES LET OUT A low whistle,
eyes a surprised round
as he stared at me.

"Holy shit," I cursed in awe.
"No kidding—can you give me tips?
That was some rom-com level
kissing right there."

Sprawling across the couch
I ignored his teasing.
I prayed it was teasing,
I wasn't about to
makeout with oranges so my
brother could level up his game.

"What am I going to do?" I drawled.
"Why do you have *to do* anything?" James asked.
"Could it really work?" I questioned.
James shrugged, "Why not?"
"We come from very different worlds,"

I reminded him.

"Sure, but that's *nothing*," James insisted.
"Darcy grew up rich, so did Bianca–although,
Darcy is rich people rich, but she's from Detroit,
not Neptune. It'll be fine."

"Maybe..." I murmured.
"You have to at least see it through," James insisted,
I knew he was right, of course he was,
but I'd be an idiot if I wasn't intimidated.
Everything about Darcy,
life, friends, career,
even the way she kissed was elevated;
better than anything I'd ever known.
I felt James in my peripheral
giving me the *don't overthink this*
stare and I knew I had to be making that
thinking man face only my mother found cute.

"She said to call her," James said,
"So you *should* call her."
"Isn't now too soon?"

James shrugged.
"Too soon isn't a real thing,
I practically friend zoned myself
thinking I had to wait."

I picked up my phone,

promptly setting it back down
Had it even been ten minutes
since she'd been here?
God, I felt batty—
but in the best way.
I decided to text her instead.
At the very least,
I could officially ask her out.
**ME:** Can I take you out Friday?
**DARCY:** I don't know, can you?
I smiled. Cheeky, brat.
**ME:** May I take you out?
**DARCY:** I'd like that.
**DARCY:** You're going to the Flint Institute of Art
next Wednesday right?

"Why are you going to FIA next Wednesday?"
I belted out to James.
His voice echoed from the kitchen
where I heard the tinkling of utensils
as he fixed up a bowl of stir fry.
"Local student exhibit, Bianca owns
an art gallery in Detroit, she's seeking
undiscovered talent to promote family
business, I think."

I texted Darcy back confirming
my presence and to my surprise
she kept writing me:
What we streamed,

what we dreamed,
we chatted about it all,
and the more I got to know her casually
the more I wanted to know her intimately;
and see her sooner than three days
without any interruptions.

# 16

I'D BEEN COMING HERE
    since I was a child.
    It'd be easy to say
    that everyone in the city
    got to come to FIA but
    that would be a privileged
    infused lie.

    Inner cities have the same crux,
    all of the resources,
    all of the hidden gems,
    rarely used or seen
    by local folks;
    hidden under the assumption
    of accessibility.
    It always surprises a tourist
    to hear many New Yorkers
    have never seen the Statue of Liberty.

    Ironically,
    my younger siblings

(with the exception of Mario,
who'd stayed at Pizza Palace)
were acting like they'd never
been anywhere, let alone
an art museum, and I was
one more crude joke,
about boobs, asses, or farts,
away from hauling them back
to Pizza Palace for penance.
We'd been saddled with siblings
determined to crash our proverbial party.
James was embarrassed,
hyper fixating on every
exhibit we went through.

Bianca seemed to be making
the most of it, trailing behind James,
stopping when he stopped
commenting when he commented.
We never should have been
live-in nannies.
but now,
after moving out,
there was no excuse.

James was too nice but *I wasn't*,
and despite his peacemaker ways,
it was past time for our parents
to be responsible for their own children.

I caught Leo crip walking
around a bronze sculpture
and I shot him a piercing look
that stopped him dead in his steps.

Darcy was a few feet away,
she looked stoic,
her face set to resting as she studied
a landscape with a pinkening sky,
a line of piercing gold-red-orange
breaking through the tree line,
entitled sunrise-sunset.

She turned, catching me
mid-stride to her side;
her face breaking into the easy smile
I was accustomed to when we were alone.

Shoulder to shoulder
We stood for a moment
fingers interlocked
as we gazed together.
"Is it a sunrise or a sunset?" I asked.
"Both," Darcy said fixing her gaze
once again to the painting.
"Beginnings are always an end."
I thought for a moment, then asked:
"You're of the opinion we should
always be bold enough to change
or try something new?"

"Exactly," Darcy agreed.
I heard an inappropriate cackle
and let our hands drop back
to our own sides.
I had about sixty seconds
before Leo (now with Kit in tow)
started up again.
Darcy's eyes flitted over my shoulder,
with an acknowledging expression
that she knew I was bailing,
hauling my brothers home
while the night was still salvageable,
for Bianca and James' sake at the very least.

"See you tomorrow for coffee?" I asked.
Darcy nodded. "Wouldn't miss it."

**17**

—.—

A GAME OF FOOT and mouse
   under the table by Darcy
   wasn't what I would have ever
   predicted happening, honestly,
   neither was having silent reading
   dates over cliche-quoted mugs
   yet, here we were, and it was *perfect*.

   Footsies simple as it was,
   was distracting nonetheless.
   The gentle tease of that, flirty caress
   made me want to scoop her up
   onto my lap and–read.
   Yes, I wanted to help her
   turn the pages of her book
   one, by one, by one,
   yes–I'd stick with that.
   Darcy seemed sad when I began
   to gather my things to leave.
   I couldn't resist semi-quickly
   kissing the pout off her lips;

nor the pep in my step knowing
she wanted to spend time with me
as much as I wanted to with her.

# 18

—·—

Legend has it,
    Petal Pushers was a
    hood business long before
    the brick and mortar storefront.

    Charlotte's parents
    started it in the fifties,
    a non-profit beautification gig
    handing out pots, plants, nutrient-rich soil,
    for flower boxes and easements,
    filling graveyard buckets,
    that budded, then blossomed
    and then Petal Pushers bloomed
    into a fully fledged flower empire.
    Flora the people for the people.

    Now it was was our Lady Liberty
    of the mini-mart;
    a beautiful bronze beacon,
    as symbolic as it was
    a literal reminder of what

creativity and ambition could become
when entangled.


I walked across the mart
to find Charlotte browsing bouquets
behind the desk on the cashier-iPad.
As I got closer, I saw they
weren't just any arrangements,
they were *wedding flowers.*


"Something you want to tell me?"
I teased, rousing her from her digital peruse.
She looked up at the sound of my voice,
her face lighting up watts
as she bolted up.


"Actually yes, I haven't seen you
to tell you; I'm getting married!"


I was stunned. "To who?"

# 19

THERE WAS A TIME where
I would have known
everything about Charlotte
but the older we got the
more casual—a natural
friend zone.

She narrowed her eyes.
"John, who else would it be?"
"The boring—rich guy?" I stammered.

Charlotte waved a hand to shush me.
"He's not *that* rich," she insisted.

"No, just *that* boring," I countered.
"He's rich enough to not be relatable.
How will you two get along?"

She pressed her lips together
into a thin angry line–she was pissed.
I'd said too much, pushed too far,

punched the bear rather than poked.

"Are you here for flowers
or fulfilling a need to harass
hard working people?" Charlotte snapped.

I smirked.
"Both—but truly. I need a favor.
Can you squeeze me and a plus one
to your 6PM floral class tonight?"

"You know we have a tight budget for those—"

"I'll pay for our supplies."

I could tell Charlotte had no
on the tip of her angry tongue
but would say yes out of loyalty.

"How am I going to *squeeze* you in if
we're already at capacity?"

"We'll be flower-arranging-flies on a wall," I promised.
"Fine," Charlotte finally relented. "Is your *date*
the girl you dropped at Rollhaven?"

That moment felt like years ago
I'd forgotten it'd even happened,
let alone that Charlotte had been there.
It was pretty hilarious looking back.

"Yes, I'm bringing Darcy," I replied.

"Aren't you worried she won't understand you?"
Charlotte quipped. "I mean, not at first of course,
but eventually?"

"I shouldn't have pried," I apologized.
"I'm just saying," Charlotte continued, "you'd get some
helpful perspective looking in the mirror."
"Noted, thanks Charman—"
"Don't you *Charmander* me."

I knew she wasn't mad, not really,
but she one-hundred-percent
meant what she'd said.
Admittedly, I could correlate
the hypocrisy of me judging
her and needing her help
planning an elaborate date;
it was a classic case of
rules for thee, not for me.

# 20

I MADE MY
way through the day
to Great Giant
for dinner,
reserved seats with
four cards each
at Bingo Balls.
I couldn't think of
anything,
or anyone,
I'd put more effort into.

**21**

I REGRETTED EVERY ILL-ADVISED
    sense of confidence I'd ever felt
    as I parked my charcoal Jeep Patriot
    in front of Darcy's rental.
    I'd gotten the picture that
    they were in town on business,
    that her family owned a company
    focused on property development
    but I wasn't sure fully what that meant.
    I now knew: it meant the best of the best,
    even in a short-term rental.
    I sent Darcy an *I'm here* text,
    then thumbed *property developers* into
    the search bar on my phone:
    property management,
    marketing and sales,
    design and construction,
    project financing and
    land acquisition.
    The last category rang a bell;
    Darcy's business was all about properties.

Was that what'd led her to the mini-mart?

*ding, ding, ding!*

Bells rang in my head as
all the pieces clicked into place.
I felt nervous now;
here I was, thinking I was
showing off the heart
of my community but this date
might make her want to *buy* it.

Fuck.
The bells turned to sirens,
my heart beating at an alarmed
pace thumping in my chest
like the old basketballs
I'd tossed around behind
Pizza Palace as a kid,
the deflated thud
a dead ringer that the ball
couldn't be thrown high enough
to get it through the hoop.

A tap at my window
centered me momentarily,
and I saw Darcy leaned over
waving as she peered into the car.
*Just drive off*, an intrusive
voice whispered, *either she'll*

*want to sell out the mini-mart*
*or worse she won't see value*
*in it at all.*

My gut wrenched,
but as scared as I was,
all the trillion of outcomes
being with Darcy could lead to,
I couldn't walk away
and live with not knowing.
I let her in and as she slid into
the adjacent passenger seat
the car filling with her presence,
the energy of our budding romance,
the shared aspiration that
this time it would be different,
gave me enough momentum to
shove away my anxiety fueled fears
and just *trust*.
Darcy grinned excitedly.
"Where's our first stop?" she asked.
"To get you some well-deserved flowers."

# 22

DARCY PLACED HER HAND in mine,
   intertwining our fingers,
   as we walked into Petal Pushers.
   The storefront was a tight squeeze,
   but as we followed the path
   entrenched with floral displays,
   the space opened into a small
   garage used to unload in another life.
   I'd only come to these
   classes in the beginning
   to be supportive of Charlotte
   and in my head, I imagined
   them filled with mee-maws and
   pops but it was mostly young people
   and almost split in half
   between genders.

   A handful of tables were arranged
   stools stuck underneath for sitting
   but most people were standing
   already beginning to tinker with

the six f-lettered blueprint to bouquets:
Floaters,
Finishers,
Foliage,
Focal,
Filler and
Foundation.
I only knew because it was
on a poster filled with roses.

Roses always reminded me
of Tupac's rose
*that grew from concrete,*
*proving nature wrong*
*by keeping its dreams,*
*and breathing fresh air,*
*growing from concrete*
*when no one else ever cared.*

Resilience.
That's what this place,
the mini-mart,
as a whole,
meant to me.

Darcy gave my arm
an excited tug.
"A floral arrangement class?"
I smiled and nod.
steering us to the last

free spot at a table.

"Looks like everyone's here,
let's get started then!"
Charlotte chirped from
the front of the garage.

"We've got some newbies tonight,
who can tell them the six f-words?"

I raised my hand quickly.
Darcy giving me an impressed expression,
while Charlotte gave me an amused one.

**23**

—·—

ABOUT AN HOUR LATER,
    flowers in hand,
    we trotted next door
    to Great Giant
    and we traded bouquets
    for cooking aprons.

    Self-taught Chef Bruce
    wore a cap and a toque;
    store manager by day,
    home-grown-gardener-cook by night;
    weekends he taught
    free cooking classes,
    using about-to-expire meats
    and produce pulled from
    above-ground garden-beds
    (watered with roof rain
    dripping into gutters,
    funneled into gravel
    filled barrels with spigots
    and hoses)

lined up in rows
behind the store.

We cooked,
we ate,
we fell more in *like*.

# 24

—·—

"THIS HAS BEEN NICE," Darcy said
    as we stepped into the warm
    night air, hooking a curved
    finger under my chin,
    pulling me down for a kiss.

"You're not tired, are you?" I teased.
"Is there more?" she asked
"Just one more stop," I promised.
"Lead the way."

I pivoted to head to Bingo Balls,
but Darcy caught my hand to stop me.

"Tonight's been really fun and sweet
and showed a lot of effort. Thank you."
Darcy's deeply earnest eyes
made me wonder:
had no one taken the time,
had no one willingly given intimacy
born of vulnerability rather than lust?

I was on the way to feeling sad

for past Darcy, but realized

no one had done this for me either.

So many firsts,

so many reasons

to pray this time was real.

# 25

"Invite me in,"
Darcy rasped in a quick
breath between kisses.
I cupped her face—
knowing deep down
that if we did this,
if we got this close,
shared our truest selves,
there'd be no going back.
Either we'd win or bust.

I searched her eyes
for some hint of how
deep her affection was,
needing to gauge if
we were close or
miles apart in how we felt.
*"Elijah,"* Darcy said,
hearing her say my name
spurred me into action.

I couldn't care about the future,
*now* is all there is.


"I want you to come in, Darcy."

# 26

— · —

DECADENT
    The word sang on my tongue
    with every lick
    and every moan she sighed
    tilting her closer
    to the edge until
    she unwittingly let go.

    incandescent
    I couldn't hold back
    and she didn't want
    me to
    I didn't want me to either
    so I obliged our desires
    fists above her head
    our hands gripped each other
    crumpling the sheets
    as I seated myself fully
    between her quivering thighs
    over and over again
    her pulse on the tip of my

tongue as I kissed her neck
and listened to her sing my
name in a breathy tone
I'd never wanted to forget.

**27**

I SLEPT HARD,
Darcy curled up
in my arms like
she belonged,
like she'd always been there,
and when she began to stir
I let myself wake up too;
unsure what to anticipate.

This was new territory,
not *new new,* but it'd been
a while in general, and even
longer since I'd let
anyone actually *sleep*
with me.

I'm sure there was
affordable therapy
somewhere ready to help me
sort through all the
whys and hows, but I was

focused on my current truth,
I was entangled with the feeling,
knowing I was on an erotically charged
interview upon which the success
of my performance was contingent
on how Darcy told me:
good morning.

I was spiraling down
a hillside of possibility
tumbling closer to
an unflattering bit of insecurity,
fueled by the acute awareness
that I was *really* into Darcy;
and desperately wanted mutuality.

Darcy began to wake,
giving me a sleepy smile
as she slid down my torso,
nipping and kissing
until she reached her route's
(obvious) destination.

She took me almost fully
with her mouth,
making me bite my fist
in surprise to keep from
moaning her name;
working me over so
confidently I unraveled

with a quickness
I was sure would come
across as too eager but
*these violent delights,*
*have violent ends*
and the victorious smirk
marked across her face
as she slid back up to kiss me
told me everything I needed to know.

28

"Good morning," Darcy said.
Her energy exuded confidence.
She *knew* she had me and as sexy
as it was, to be honest,
I was a little shook
and the safest way
for me to deal
with being out of my
comfort zone was to
pretend I wasn't, in fact,
out of my comfort zone.

I kissed her forehead and
watched her full figure
slide down my chest
as I half sat up.

"Hungry?" I asked.
"Famished," she replied,
her enthusiasm making me grin.
"I can't imagine why."

"Cute," she said, rolling
over to search for her shirt.

I could see it, crumbled
and somehow on my side.
I waited a moment,
watching the sheet
slink around her curves,
grazing over her hips
as she stretched,
searching her side of the bed.
She finally noticed I
was holding it and
gave me a *haughty* look
that had me laughing.

She reached for the shirt
and I easily moved it
out of her reach.
Her laugh
tinkled through the
morning air.

I shook my head at her
playfully.
"Pay the toll," I declared.
Darcy scooted closer,
studying me carefully.
"You don't look like a troll."
"Kiss or be nude," I teased.

She kissed me with such
potent veracity we almost
tumbled back to bed.

**29**

—·—

"How do you like your eggs?"
  "Scrambled is—" Darcy began to say
but her ringing phone cut her short.

Darcy sat on the couch to answer,
and I tried to tone out her voice
but her authoritative cadence
was hard to ignore.

Her tone confident,
so decisive and knowledgeable;
she sounded like a boss,
she sounded like she was discussing
development plans with *someone.*
The male voice on the other end spoke
in a snippy, domineering, yet familiar, way;
perhaps her father?

The realization that I didn't *know*
this side of Darcy struck me.
I felt I should, and internally

vowed to get to know all her sides;
the dualities of Darcy.
As soon as the call was done
Darcy came back,
perched on a bar stool and
asked me about my day-to-day routines.

"Pizza Palace doesn't
open 'til the afternoon
during the week, earlier on
the weekends as it's busier.
But I typically close every
night."

"Not last night," she teased.
I winked.

"Well, I'd love to see you
again—soon—like tonight soon,"
Darcy suggested.

"What's a normal workday
like for you?"
"It depends," Darcy said,
"but generally incredibly flexible
when you own the company."

I dropped my spatula in surprise,
It teetered around the rim before
flopping on to the stove.

"You *own* the company?"
"Perks of being the
Dead Parents Club president."

I almost dropped
my dropped spatula again.

"It's okay," Darcy said,
she reached for my hand
and squeezed it comfortingly;
the gesture made me sad,
she was used to people feeling
sorry for her, needing her,
to comfort them.
But who comforted Darcy?

"Really, Elijah, it's okay," she repeated.

"Right—of course, it just surprised me,"
I stammered quickly. "I thought that was your
Dad on the phone."

"Uncle," Darcy corrected.
"He is on the company's board,
is very involved and bitter
that he isn't in control, but is
extremely good at his job.
Which happens to be mainly,
doing what I tell him to do."

Her haughtiness
caught me off guard.

I'd always been a self-proclaimed
easy come, easy go,
level headed sort of guy,
but I wouldn't tolerate
a second mother.
I wanted a true partner
not an–albeit, extremely attractive–overload.

I nodded, but turned to plate her food
—bacon, eggs, toast, hashbrowns—
as she kept talking.

"We came here, specifically,
for potential land acquisitions;
underdeveloped areas always
have growth opportunities with
exceptional profit margins due to
poverty, price of land–"

"That's *really* what brought you
to Pizza Palace that night?" I asked.
I remembered Bianca casually mention
something along the lines of Darcy being
a developer but I didn't understand
how literal she'd been.

"Yes, we were looking at the Mini-Mart
in its entirety as an investment opportunity."

I could feel myself becoming
defensive; every breath
I took fueling my anger
rather than subduing it.

I placed her food down
and took a desperate handful
of beats to steady my temper.

"Did you know my family owns
the mini-mart and all the businesses
are our tenants?" I finally asked.

Darcy paused,
placing her fork neatly to the left
of her plate as if this conversation
needed her full attention—which granted,
it did, we were skating on notoriously thin ice.

"I knew it was owned by the Bennets
and I pieced together quickly that you
were *a* Bennet," she answered truthfully.

"It's not for sale," I quickly snapped,
full stop, I wanted this bud nipped.

Darcy raised her hands in surrender.

"I have no intention of trying to
buy the mini-mart."

"It's not *for sale*," I repeated.

I was sensing an undertone of audacity,
an everything is for sale vibe
that I found completely intolerable.

"Ok," Darcy said, watching me closely.
"Truthfully, even if it was for sale,
it wouldn't be a smart investment.
But I can promise you that I would never–"

"It wouldn't be a smart investment?"
I'd crossed the line now,
standing firmly, ten toes down
in Offended county.

Darcy picked up her fork
and began eating again
and forced a smile.

"This food is really good," she said.
"Darcy, what do you mean?"

"Elijah," she said slowly,
as if a normal speaking speed
would be too much for me to understand,
"I don't want to fight

continuing this conversation
is going to make you upset with me."

I knew right then and there
I'd gladly die on this hill.
"What did you mean, Darcy?"

My tone was sharper than I'd meant,
but she was wrong. I wasn't on the path
to being upset, I was already there, in upset park
having an upset picnic on a sunny upset day.

"Ok, truthfully, all of the business are rundown,
they'd require a lot of renovations that would
make us upside down on any investment we put in
with an extremely low return on investment rate."

I began to steam but her response
to my next question would either
lower me to a simmer
or raise me to a boil.

"Wasn't the property reviewed before you came here?" I retorted.

"A preliminary demographic review yes,"
Darcy replied, "and I had recommendations."

I thought back to that night,
to my first conversation with Darcy,
where Bianca had tried to explain

what Darcy did for a living
but had to have Darcy explain
it herself:

"Low-income housing,
community centers or
charter schools;
whatever makes sense."

"What was your recommendation?"

"To acquire land to build housing—but
after last night, I determined it wouldn't be
good for your community."

"After *last* night? You've been in town
getting to know—us—for weeks."

"I've been getting to know *you*,
and I like you a lot," Darcy said.

She reached for my hand
but I pulled away.

"Elijah?" She sounded unsure,
her voice with a hairline of a
crack on the verge of expanding,
exploding any second.

"You're the vulturous head of a

gluttonous profit-centric company,"
I spat in anger, "that has no concerns for how
their *investments* stripped communities
bare because bringing an impoverished
community to their knees was more
profitable than teaching them to
stand on their own."

"My assessment is rooted in logic –
facts not feelings," Darcy argued back.

"Of course," I scoffed,
you're ruled by logic."

"I'm not ruled by logic,
I'm aware that being
with you isn't ideal
from a social economical
point of view but that
doesn't stop or change
how I feel about you."

"Maybe it should," I snarled,
"because this conversation is
changing how I feel about you."

"That's not fair," Darcy insisted.
"I'm being honest with you,
you're being emotional with me."

"I'm being a man,
made of flesh and bone, Darcy!
Emotions and feelings,
however inconvenient for you, are
natural for us mortals."


"I have feelings–I just expressed them for–"


"Feelings centered around money, growth and
what was it, social statuses?"


Her lip quivered.


"You feel like this, us, was a mistake?" she whispered.
"Yes," I lied.


She began gathering her things
and the urge to stop her
was strong but I held
my ground and watched
her leave.


It was better to end it now,
then when I was already in love.

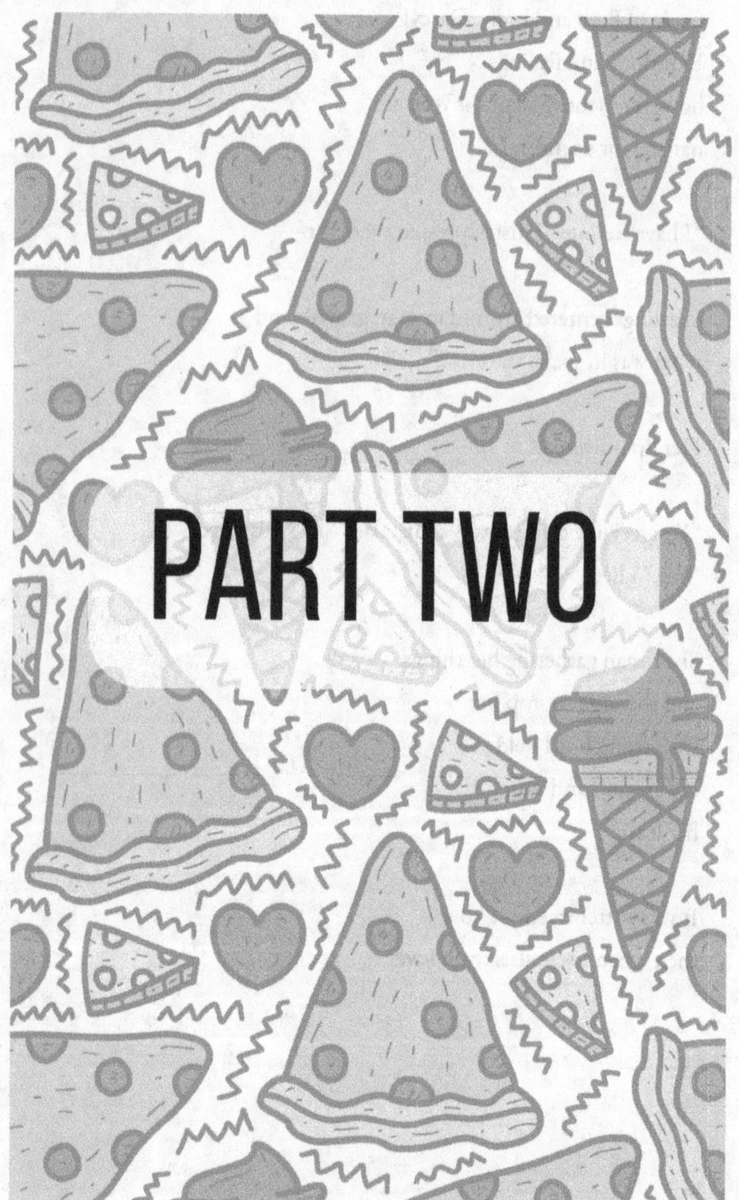

# PART TWO

## 30

—·—

**30**

"You really haven't
heard from Darcy?"
James asked for the
millionth time.

I shrugged—
a non-verbal
response was the best
I could manage.

James was gone that morning,
leaving the only truth being
whatever I told and I wasn't talking.

I had guilt,
immense regret,

fear that my emotional spillage
would saturate and ruin James'
delicate Bianca filled future;
it probably already had.

I had whiplash,
we'd gone from blazing to frigid
and I was left swirling, whirling,
from the drastic change.

The hardest thing–
the disappointment.
As time passed, I hoped
our memories faded;
they were so raw,
seared into my mind,
micro tattoos fading
but never erased.

Wasn't it for the best?
Oil and water accepting
their inability to mix.
I thought so, and yet,
a nagging part of me
was still whispering
*it could have worked.*

"Maybe it could have
worked," James said,
unknowingly echoing

my own thoughts, "it still
could."

I shook my head again,
and James relented
allowing me to focus on
placing pepperonis around
the edge of a very thin crust.

**31**

—·—

A week later,
 my premonitions
 became fruition.
 Bianca had gone
 back to the city;
 no longer responding
 to James' texts.
 Fuck.

## 32

"WHAT EXACTLY ISN'T WORKING?"
my mother, Missie Bennet,
pointedly asked.

We were sitting in the back office,
corralled by Pizza Palace receipts
and piled-high papers we'd no
longer needed but kept for the
"records" we didn't officially keep.

"This," I said, with an
exasperated flail of my arms.
"Pizza Palace?" she asked
"Not just here, everywhere
and everything."

My mom pushed her readers
to the top of her head
and crossed her arms.
"Elijah, you sound like
a bitter Dr. Seuss book.

Can you tell me in
*full* complex sentences
what is wrong?"

"That's the problem," I sighed,
"I'm not sure what's wrong,
just that, nothing feels right.
Maybe it's because,
I've always towed the line
and I've never truly
done anything for myself."

"What do you want to do?"

"I don't even know
what I would want to do
if I *could* do whatever I wanted,"
I stammered, flustered,

Missie's eyes narrowed.
"Is this because it didn't work
out with those bougie city girls?
Your father was way too excited
thinking it would create
magical-status-elevating connections
but elevation is overrated;
not enough air at high altitudes,
harder to *breathe*,
harder to *work*,
harder to *see* what really matters."

I exhaled, leaning heavily into my chair
"It's impressive how you're simultaneously
right and wrong."

"Look, Elijah," Missie said,
"if you want more, do more.
You're vital but you're not a prisoner
Decide what you want.
We'll figure it out."

"I do love it here—
I just want *more*," I explained.

"How about this:
Bubbles is yours;
income would be enough to replace
what you make at Pizza Palace,
you can set your own hours,
fire or keep the current staff,
find another mini-mart project;
I love what you've done with Bingo Balls,
and the Giant Garden,
you've got talent, kiddo!
No denying that, you just need direction."
I liked that idea.
There were more renovations needed
above the store fronts
either to rent out or turn into *something*.
My wheels started spinning; There was

even the basement below Brick Busters
could become a single screen movie theatre
with the right elbow-grease.

"A few more *supervised* work hours
would be good for Leo too,
help tire him out and shorten his leash.
If ever there was a child designed
to sharpen my saw it'd be our Leo,"
Missie murmured with a shake of her head.
"I remember those days,"
I said, chuckling, "he's a good kid,
he'll be alright."

"No," Missie said, with a tired sigh,
"you and James were good kids,"
"Leo is incorrigible at best on a good day."

"Back to business," I said with a renewed
sense of vigor, "what's our project budget like?"

"Whoa, Garret Morgan, calm down."

"You've got jokes,
but I'll take being compared
to an inventor as the compliment
that it is."

Missie smiled.
"I meant it how you took it, son.

Money is tight,
but we've got about eight thousand
we could allocate to projects.
My advice:
make that money work
for you and piggyback off profits."

I was surprised by
that large of an amount.
"Can we really afford
that much?"

"We can as long as
I continue to manage
our finances and
don't plan on retiring soon.

"Ma—" I began, but she
waved a hand to shush me.
"It's fine, Elijah, just don't squander time,
live a life you're proud to live."

**33**

I LIKED PAINTING,
  always had.

Not landscapes or fruit,
not even puppies or sunsets,
just walls.

It was a clean start,
a literal fresh coat;
the most chemical-smelling
induced new beginning
you could ever imagine.

I cracked open a window
and leaned on the sill.
Palms cruddy from
all the dusty dirt,
but my face felt clean
as the morning wind blew
across my brow and cheeks.

"You look like a ghetto
Rose from *Titanic*," I heard
Charlotte's voice tease
from the entrance way.
She'd let herself in to
the studio apartment
I was rehabbing
(this time) above
Brick Buster's.

"You here to paint
or to gab?" I asked.
"Well at least you look happy for once.
Too much primer, I suppose?"

I laughed.
"Just the right amount."

"Really opens the mind,"
Charlotte giggled. "I can't stay long,
because if I do you'll put me to work,
I just wanted to formerly
invite you to my engagement party."

"I responded *no*
to your electronic Invite."
Charlotte raised an eyebrow.
"You did, hence why
I'm asking in person."

"I don't know if it's a good—"

"It *is* a good idea. That's why I'm insisting."

"It's all the way in the city," I argued.

"*All the way in the city* is an hour drive."

"It feels like another world entirely," I muttered.

"I'm sure it would," Charlotte quipped,
"since you stay submerged
in our small-big-town,
but change of pace is
good for the mind-body-soul.
Plus, your mom
told my mom,
who told me that you've been kind of—"

"Okay, fine," I agreed quickly
hoping to stop her from
telling me the three-person-removed
*tea* started by one half of my
traitorous creators.

Charlotte gave a victorious whoop and wink.
"You make it too easy,
that gossip was a bluff.

"Fuck," I cursed.

"No take-backsies!" Charlotte sang
as she left, "see you tonight!"

**34**

—·—

I'D ALWAYS BEEN IMPARTIAL
   to the city.
   It was funny-ironic since
   I lived in a city, but locals
   knew the distinction between
   *our city* and *the city*.

   Flint was a satellite,
   a theoretical moon
   floating around a bigger moon
   like Detroit or Grand Rapids
   big enough to not be small
   but comparatively still small
   side-by-side to other cities.

   Still, it was *my city*.
   I was comfortable here.
   It was familiar and if not safe,
   safe-adjacent, but Charlotte's soiree
   celebrating her engagement
   was in *the city* and I didn't want to go.

I didn't belong there, yet a promise,

any way you slice it, is still a promise.


Exasperated by all my inabilities,

I slapped my roller down into the paint pan;

Just another mess I'd have to clean up.

**35**
—·—

It hadn't occurred to me
    that she would be here.
    I'd done my best to block
    any reminiscent thoughts of her
    that I hadn't even thought.
    Clearly, she knew Charlotte's fiancé,
    and that guilty smirk Charlotte sent
    my way meant she'd known it too.
    I'd been treacherously tricked.
    Now, Darcy was coming for me,
    far more than beautiful,
    right through the arrays of
    dancing people,
    past hors d'oeuvres
    and pretty glasses
    filled with tiny bubbles,
    straight to me,
    and I regretted my rebellious
    stick-it-to-Charlotte-attitude
    when I'd dressed casually.
    I'd felt empowered by

a little *fuck you* to my life long friend.
Now in a sweater and jeans
against this *Gatsby* backdrop
I felt simple, dull, grunge in
a miserable wet cat kind of way.

I should run,
barrel roll out a window even,
but I was stunned,
a sailor lured to his siren;
too far gone to look away.
I didn't want to be saved.
I was at the rocks and she
was above me on the shore.

"Dance with me," she ordered,
equally obnoxious as it was attractive.
I hated my knee jerk reaction to agree.

"Elijah, please," she said softly.

I could resist *that* even less than bossy Darcy.
Soft, pliable, compliant,
bringing up memories
or other times she'd been
trusting and compliant
with me.

"Fine," I grumbled.
She quickly grabbed my hand

as if she knew if she didn't lead I'd run.

**36**

## I still wasn't convinced

RUNNING WAS A BAD idea;
   smarter than being hypnotized
   by the sway of her hips
   as she moved us deep
   into the dance floor,
   submerged within a sea
   of slow dancing bodies,
   wasting no time pulling me close.

   Darcy's lips looked as soft
   as I remembered.
   For a moment I forgave her,
   fantasizing about how I would
   pull her closer until her body
   was flush against mine,
   tell her I missed her,
   kiss her as if no harsh words
   or time had passed between us,

but how could I?

It didn't matter how I felt
or how good she smelled.
Nothing socially or economically
had changed between us,
or *would, could, should.*
Pick your verb, it didn't matter which.

"I know you don't want
to talk to me," Darcy said,
the earnest look in her eyes
made me pull her closer,
if only so I wouldn't have to look
at her while she spoke
and she couldn't see
how it was making me feel;
cheek to cheek,
we swayed a slow beat,
her voice humming below my ear.

## 37

"I SAID A LOT of things poorly

that I want to clarify," Darcy began.

"You couldn't just call?" I asked.

"Would you have answered?"

"Did you tell Bianca about our fight?" I blurted out.


Darcy pulled back abruptly,

surprised but answered candidly,

"Yes, I did."

"And then Bianca ghosted James?"

"Yes," Darcy confirmed, "but only because

she believed him to be impartial."

"Impartial?" I snapped. "He's clearly in love with her!".

"How would she *know* that? He barely talks."

"He's shy!" I stammered.


"Elijah,

I want to apologize,

to explain myself,

to hopefully salvage what we *have*."

I pushed away from her.
"Let me get this straight,
my brother isn't good enough for Bianca,
but I'm too irresistible to pass up?"

"I didn't say that. I *like* James."
"Then why interfere?" I pushed.

Darcy threw her hands up.
"I didn't intentionally—"

"But you did," I interrupted, "you,
Darcy Fitzgerald, are responsible for
my brother's current and future states of unhappiness."

"How can I make this right?" Darcy asked.
I narrowed my eyes. "You're serious?"
"Of course, I am, I never intend—"

"There you both are!" Charlotte's
voice cut through crowd as she beelined
to us; her eyes darted between Darcy and I.

"You're being nice, right?"
Charlotte asked me, specifically.

Darcy couldn't even look at me.

"I think I'm going to call it a night," Darcy whispered.
Charlotte was astonished. "No! Why?"

"Stay—I'll go if this is too uncomfortable," I offered.
"Everyone stays, and everyone gets a drink," Charlotte ordered.

As I reluctantly nodded,
Darcy made an apologetic smile
so sad I lost the will to fight or be mad.
I'd never admit that though.

# 38

A FEW SHOTS LATER

I felt (temporarily) better.

It's a science.

## 39

DARCY WAS NOW AVOIDING *me*,
maybe because I'd finally succeeded in
freezing her out
or perhaps was too fearful
of my wrath to come any closer.

It sucked seeing Darcy.
I'd missed all of her,
but I shouldn't have—
she'd made it crystal clear:
I wasn't good enough.
I refused to be something
someone settled for.

*But still,* I thought,
my glance turning to stare,
*it couldn't hurt to look, right?*
I watched her dance,
mingle and eventually
sit at the same large
round table as me.

I was, unironically,
barely talking to anyone,
clearly distraught over
—what was it now—
our third argument?
I snorted to myself,
wondering why I was keeping track.

"Are you okay?" Darcy asked.
How loud was that snort?
Maybe I was drunker than I realized.

When I didn't answer
she scooted a few chairs over,
placed her hand on mine.

"Elijah?"

I looked up,
facing her fully now.
Her skin looked so soft,
I didn't bother resisting
trailing my thumb along
the side of her jaw,
like I had once before.

Her eyes fluttered
closed, just for a moment,
unable to stop herself

from leaning into my touch.

"I don't communicate well,"
I mumbled, my hand falling away.
Darcy caught it with her own.
"You can't drive home tonight," she assessed.
"Why?" I teased. "Have you missed me?"
A blush crept across her cheeks,
a shy smile across her face.

"You're drunk," she murmured.
I sighed, stretching big. "I am."
Darcy gave my hand a pat,
"You're staying with me tonight."
"Force proximity," I smirked, "another great trope."
Darcy rolled her eyes, barely biting back a smile.
"I can't agree to sleeping with you–
"Staying with me," Darcy corrected.
"Either or, really," I said, "until I know,
what kind of couch you have."

Darcy gave my hand a squeeze
before pulling me up from my seat
and wrapping her arms around my waist.

"It's better than yours," she teased.

Engulfing her in a hug,
I nuzzled the crown of her head.
"I'm sure it is, bougie," I teased too,

mirroring her energy.
"You're just a little shorter than me.
You don't want a tall guy?
You know, someone with
manlier height proportions."

Darcy laughed and pinched
the side of my ribs.
"You're a silly lush."

"Are you saying
I'm silly hot or a silly drunk
because I almost never drink
but I'm good looking daily."

Darcy shook her head,
tightening her grip
around me and began to walk.
I let her guide me,
the floor squished like taffy
with each step.
"Come on, Fabio," Darcy urged,
"let's get you to my excellent couch."

"Ew, no, I'm Michael P. Jordan
or Edris Elba or even that prison
model with the gorgeous eyes."

"Your eyes are brown."

"And Fabio is white, what's your point?"

"I have missed you, Elijah," Darcy confessed.
I pushed an awkward kiss into her hair.
"Me too," I drawled.

# 40

I FELL ASLEEP IN the car,
    my next conscious thought
    being Darcy nudging me awake.
    My nap sobered me up
    (marginally) as I was
    able to "casually" stroll
    to the building's elevator.

    The entrance way was *nice*,
    bronze mailboxes encased
    in art deco wall paper or tiles;
    too tipsy to know for sure.

    I made a low whistle as
    we passed into the elevator
    Darcy laughed, shaking her head.
    Her apartment was gorgeous too,
    very tastefully put together.
    I low key fall asleep to HGTV
    every night—it was kind of my
    thing—so even tired and mildly

intoxicated, I could appreciate
the restored dark herringbone floors
in contrast to the white kitchen
and minimalistic furniture.

"It's beautiful," I murmured.
"You said bougie wrong," Darcy teased.
I caressed her cheek
as I plopped down on her
tan leather couch.
"I'm too hard on you," I confessed,
"a mix of insecurity and jealous,
I think, but *everyone* can't be poor.
That would *suck*."
Darcy laughed, light an airy
like a harp or something
equally lovely, she felt like home,
put me at ease–all at once.
She knelt, beginning the task
of remove my shoes, the act of service
making me emotional and weighted down
by unworthiness, as if I didn't deserve
to be taken care of.

Darcy gave my thigh a reassuring
rub and I realized then
I was actually crying.
I quickly wiped my face.
"It's fine," Darcy assured me.
But it really wasn't, suddenly

(or not so suddenly)
I'd realized a million reasons
to be sad.

I felt the couch shift as Darcy got close,
nuzzling on top of me until
our legs and arms intertwined,
entangled beneath a soft throw
I somehow in my pissed state knew
was pure alpaca wool from the Andes.
"Lying on you won't make you barf,
will it?"
I shook my head
even though I wasn't sure,
willing to risk it all to
have her in my space,
the weight of her body
pressed soothingly on top of mine.
I held her tight,
breathing in the reassurance
her presence brought me,
pushing away the truth that
I knew I didn't deserve it.

# 41



WE WOKE UP EXACTLY
  how we'd fallen asleep,
  together.

  I laid with her,
  enjoying the dream
  just a little bit longer
  before reality woke me up,
  that a little voice whispering
  *it would always be like this.*
  I wish I was convinced.

  As Darcy began to stir,
  I untangled myself
  fleeing to the bathroom,
  then marching to the kitchen
  to avoid her,
  the phantom *us* always lingering,
  leering from the shadows
  between past and present.

I couldn't help thinking
about the last time we'd been
together in a kitchen
it ended so badly—I never
thought we'd be in one together again.


"Good morning," Darcy finally murmured.


The hesitation in her tone
felt like an omission
that she was on eggshells, too.
Neither of us wanting to be
the catalyst of another quarrel.

# 42

"You want some coffee?"
Darcy asked, breezing past me
to the unnaturally clean Chemex
adjacent to the stove.

"Have you ever even used it?"
Darcy smirked over her shoulder.
"I'm not *that* privileged," she said,
stretching to reach the coffee bag
from the cupboard.

"It's just really clean," I explained.
"My governess taught me
commoner life skills, you know,
so I could be more relatable."
"Is that so?" I said,
reaching around her to
retrieve the coffee bag
she'd pushed further out
of reach with each attempt.
I handed it to her

before retreating
to the opposite counter.
"You wanna go get breakfast too?"
Darcy asked, "I wouldn't dare

ask you to cook again."

I knew she was teasing,
trying to lighten
our unresolved energy
but her words creaked
within my mind,
pulling at me in a way
that twisted my frustration
into guilt.

I offered a half-assed apology.
"I shouldn't have spoken
to you the way I did."

"Nor I to you," she replied.

"Yet we *both* did," I sighed.

We grew silent then,
watching the coffee drip
through the filter,
little splashes that felt
like a tick and a tock
as it filled and filled,
both of us waiting

on the other,
neither willing to be vulnerable.
Both of us, or at least myself,
reminiscing a romanticized idea
of what *couldn't* have been.

She poured my coffee into
a thermal travel cup,
ushering me to the door
with a sad smile
and cheeky comment
about sending me a return label
so I could send the cup back.

## 43

—·—

I WAS CLEARLY IN love with her
   and it seemed like she was
   at minimum in like with me
   all those long stares
   and sad eyes she'd given me;
   not to mention, curling up on me
   all night like I was the only place
   she preferred to be, everywhere else
   were just places she existed.

I pushed her from my mind,
   even though I was fully aware
   I wasn't over her and until we
   were both done—this *thing* wouldn't
   be done either.

We were in romantic limbo.
Maybe it could be different this time.
*It wouldn't be.*
How do you know?
*I know.*

You can't know for sure.
*I just have to—*


a sputter in the engine,

a blaring orange symbol on my dash,

and ominous grey smoke emerging from the hood

jolted me out of my monologue argument

and back to the undeniable.

*Just fucking fantastic.*

Even my car felt reluctant to leave

as if it was suddenly sentient,

mocking me for being so foolish.

**44**
—•—

Charlotte hadn't answered my call,

but Darcy had.

After digging out my peeling AAA card,

my car was being towed

and I was rescued;

swooped back to upper class.

Mechanics wouldn't even peek

under my hood until Monday,

meaning I'd be here at least that long too,

living out the legendary forced proximity trope.

My new Roman Empire?

Tropes were best when they remained

in my books, not in my life.


I'd been hesitant to call,

even more hesitant to stay again;

one third because I didn't want give in,

two thirds because I *wanted* to give in,

a three thirds because I was wholly afraid

we'd implode again.

My heart wasn't graded for

multiple combustions.

Darcy had insisted I stay
with her, not in a hotel
with a polite reassurance
to keep things platonic.
Her smirk as she said it
was dangerous territory in itself,
a light-hearted flirty tease
that made me feel ruined by her,
my resolve melting away
minute by minute
until I was able to admit that
even if we weren't for forever,
I desperately wanted her right *now*.

I couldn't help but think
—which clearly was a problem—
the universe was giving me a carrot,
a prettily wrapped mulligan
who clearly wasn't as over us as I'd fathomed.
If I could muster the courage
to let my heart speak,
I'd hear the truth: *neither was I.*
"What do you want to do
with all this time we have?"
Darcy asked casually.

I cleared my throat awkwardly
flustered because I was

hallucinating innuendos
where only politeness was audible.
"It's barely noon," Darcy continued,
ignoring my awkwardness.
"We could go exploring,
show off my all favorite spots of the city."
"Sure," I said, forcing a casual
indifferent shrug. "Lady's choice."
Darcy eyed me suspiciously.
"What?" I stammered.
"What to your *what?*" she replied.
"What?" I asked, genuinely confused.
"You're being–not normal," Darcy accused.
"I just wasn't anticipating this," I said quietly.
"Cars never seem to do what we expect." Darcy teased.

## 45

WE ENDED UP AT Blackstone's
a down-town smokehouse
with dimmed dangling lights
and dark wood floors
framed by burnt clay bricks.
The chatter of voices,
clanks of dishes,
and live music
was a genre all in itself.

"This is really nice," I exclaimed,
bumping my shoulder to hers
to emphasize my sincerity.
Darcy grinned,
looping our arms,
linking us together,
resting her cheek
on my shoulder,
gazing up at the stage,
listening to the band play *Blue Monk*
a mural of contentment

painted across her face.

Tilting her head up,
leaning in close to my ear
and said softly:
"The piano player is my brother."

I was taken aback,
realizing I knew nothing.

I'd been so infatuated,
so eager to share
I'd forgotten to receive.
I had a sinking feeling,
our fight was caused by me
talking at her
rather than with her.

"He's brilliant," I told her.
"He is," she agreed, nuzzling closer.

"It's been just the two of us
since our father passed.
My uncle looked after me,
but I always looked after George."

I caught her brush a tear away;
a quick breath of a moment
I would have missed if I'd blinked.

The set and she hopped to her feet.
"Come meet him," she said,
tugging me up behind her
as she took off for the stage.
"He's been bugging me to
introduce you for a while now."

"He knows about me?"
I asked surprised.

Darcy smirked over her shoulder,
a habit I was finding I adored.
"Everyone knows about you," she said.

George's face lit when he saw her
and he motioned for us to join him.
But rather than come to us he sat
back down at the keys and began
to play.

"Oh no," Darcy said smiling.
"Oh yes," he insisted.
"George—"
"Just one song, please?"
Darcy relented,
taking the microphone,
she began to sing.

**46**

—·—

IT WAS MAGIC, HEARING
her voice flit and fly
between harmonies and melodies.

Darcy was at home
surrounded by awed listeners,
tucked safely into memories
for so long not remembered
but summoned when she sang.

George hugged her tight
when the song was done
and I wondered how long
they'd been singing together.

Darcy ushered him over
to the wall I was posted up on
and gave my hand a squeeze.

"George," she began
cheeks still flushed from singing,

"This is Elijah."

His smile exploded,

hitting me too,

staining my own face

with a smirk.

"This is *Elijah*!"

"Sure is," I said awkwardly.

He shook my hand firmly.

"Good to meet you. If you don't

have plans, let's grab dinner.

How long will you be in town?"

"At least 'til Monday," Darcy answered.

"Let's grab something tonight, yeah?"

Darcy looked to me

and I nodded.

"Does eight work?"

"Sounds good, sis."

## 47

WE HAD A COMFORTABLE silence
while Darcy drove us back.
I often felt the need to talk,
fill the void with words
meaningful or meaningless,
I just needed reverberated
sound.

But not this time,
Darcy's focus on the road
afforded me stolen glances,
my brain churning over
her actions
my actions
my ever-shifting feelings,
my ever-shifting regrets.

I had a moment's pause,
rather than rapid-fire speak
('cause that's always gone so well).

"I didn't know you sang,"
I said, finally breaking the silence.

"It'd be easy to say you never asked
but I should acknowledge
I never shared either," Darcy teased.

"I should have *asked*," I murmured.

"Don't beat yourself up," Darcy said,
as she parked, "We're still getting
to know each other. It's a process."

I took her hand in mine,
trailed my thumb across her knuckles
and began working up the nerve to
truly apologize.

But her attention was focused
on my heather black t-shirt.
"You don't have any *clothes*."

I blinked.

"I mean, you're marooned
until your car is fixed but,
I just realized you wouldn't
have packed a weekend bag."

I tugged at my shirt,

"I keep an emergency change
of clothes, like a gentlemen."

"What happens after that?"

"Good point," I conceded.

Darcy leaned over the armrest
and fisted my emergency shirt
tugging me gently into her orbit.

"What trope is it when the
hot rich brat makes you
wait naked while she
washes all your clothes?"

I purred.
"The best one."

Her eyes fluttered to my lips,
"Is that so?"

I nodded eagerly
and she laughed
moving away,
but I hooked a finger
gently under her chin,
shifting her back to me.

Once she was close,

curving my hand around
the nape of her neck,
I tilted her head back
'til we were eye-to-eye.

Darcy took a surprised breath,
melting into my light touch
as if she'd been waiting,
wanting me,
to break our ice
from the moment
I froze her out.

What a fool I was.

"I'm sorry," I said quietly.
"I have an idea," Darcy murmured.
"Better than me kissing you?" I asked.
"Debatable," she admitted.
"Well let's hear it," I playfully demanded.
"Ask James to join us for dinner tonight."

"Really?" I asked.
Darcy grinned and nodded.
"I'll use my *influence* for good
and get Bianca to join us."

We were a breath apart now,
Just a small shift forward
for our lips to seal

our truce with a kiss.
My phone rang.
Darcy's attention faltered
at the sound.
"Ignore it," I murmured.
"I'm not going anywhere,"
Darcy promised, "answer it;
it might be important."
I groaned but obliged.
I dug my phone out of my pocket,
James was calling.

"What are you doing tonight?"
I asked jovially as soon as I answered.
James' frantic tone was distraught.

"You have to come home," he rasped,
"Leo's been arrested."

**48**

Darcy drove me home,
  our silence uncomfortable now.
  I felt no need to talk
  when I wanted to melt
  through the car's floorboard
  and vanish into the road.

  I'd judged her so harshly
  on much less,
  and now she knew her concerns,
  at the very least, were valid,
  if not worse than she imagined
  and with a fifty-eight minutes
  worth of highway ahead of us,
  I had time to deep-dive into dwelling.

**49**

WHEN I MADE IT home,
  Darcy followed me in,
  up the back stairs to my
  childhood home above Pizza Palace.
  Missie thanked her immediately
  for bringing me home,
  for being such a good friend.
  Darcy told her it was no trouble
  as she hugged her back.
  My mother took a breath,
  preparing to say more,
  but a whooping bellow from
  my distraught father made her depart
  and our attention, and source of explanation,
  fell to James.
  Between his weary worn look,
  the chaotic background noise
  of familiar chattering, it was clear
  emotions were shredded.
  Nothing like this had ever
  happened in our household before.

James explained it all.
Leo and other local kids
took it upon themselves
to steal from Great Giant,
get drunk on stolen liquor,
fill Bubbles' dryer with pens and ranch,
rip flowers at Petal Pushers,
stuff ping pongs into Bingo Ball customers' mufflers,
and attempt to steal porn from Brick Busters
while ransacking and breaking DVDs along the way.

Leo had metamorphosed from
a good kid belonging to a good family,
to the neighborhood delinquent,
our cautionary tale,
in just *one* night.

But the worst,
most unforgivable bit,
he'd done this to
his own community.

I didn't know when Darcy had
taken my hand in hers
but she squeezed it reassuringly,
as if to remind me
everything would be okay,
but I knew in my heart
they wouldn't.

"I've got to go," Darcy said,
"Will you be alright?"
I nodded silently.
Darcy didn't looked convinced
but didn't push.
She hugged me tight,
murmuring in my ear to call her
when I was ready to talk,
but the tear-soaked spots
on my shirt felt like farewell.

# 50

MY FATHER WASTED NO time
pouncing once Darcy was gone.
"Son," Monte said, "let's talk in the den."
I followed him willingly,
but the goodwill turned mud
as he began to berate me
with questions about *Darcy*;
specifically about her
wealth and connections,
emphasizing his distaste that
I'd let that fine piece of moneybags
*get away.*

"Be a man, Elijah,
don't waste opportunities
seal the deal,
take the cow
and all the proverbial milk.
Never let someone else
have what is yours," he claimed.

"What about friendship,
companionship, loyalty,
trust, *love*? Everything isn't
transactional, father."
"Of course it is! Elijah, you have
the currency *she wants*. Cash in!"

"I'll never understand what
mother saw in you," I snapped,
feeling more disgusted now
than I'd ever been.
Thank God Darcy will
at least be spared *this*.
I turned to leave,
just as my mother entered
the den.

"Monte," Missie demanded,
"put in an order for Chinese.
I need to speak with Elijah."
"We're in the middle of talking,"
Monte insisted, "and let me tell you,
he's got an attitude I don't appreciate."
"You've said enough," Missie deadpanned.

If *harrumph* was a person, it'd be my father.

"How bad is it, truly?" I asked
when we were alone.
"Bad. We're hoping to settle with tenants,

we'll be lucky if this doesn't bankrupt us.
Not just from the damages
but the reputational loss too.
The community is angry,
they feel betrayed,
they demand *retribution*."

I sat down,
rotating between
wringing my hands
and raking my hands
through my curly hair.

"I've barely touched the renovation
funds, that should help."

"Naturally," Missie said, "but
Leo will also have to be tended to.
Our family lawyer feels
the best route is to show the judge
our ownership, our accountability,
by enrolling Leo in a reforming school.
If we do not, it's likely they'll send him
either to juvie or to that horrid free
school run by the government."

"What does Leo say for himself?"
I asked gruffly.

"Teen jargon that does him no good."

My jaw clenched,
ticking at the edge in sync
to my mind's rolling credits of offenses
over the years that I was sure
had built the road to where we'd arrived.

I'd read somewhere once:
there is no rock bottom,
only death.

Was that true?
Would Leo escalate
higher and higher
until the sun finally
burnt him up?

Missie dabbed her eyes
with a crumbled tissue.
"How did we get here?" she sighed

I gave her a hug;
just as much for me
as it was for her.

**51**

IT WASN'T UNTIL MONDAY morning
that Leo was able to go
in front of a judge.

I selfishly didn't have
the stomach to go,
too afraid I'd make a scene,
either smacking the shit out of Leo
or crying like an idiot.

Instead, I stayed at Pizza Palace,
while James went to court.

Mario and Kit were forlorn and quiet.
Well, Mario was always quiet
but there was an energy about
them that oozed fear.

They were shook up,
and rightfully so.
Mario had been lost in a book

blissfully ignorant and unaware,
but Kit always knew, yet,
surprisingly enough he hadn't
been with Leo that night.
Quite the opposite,
he'd tried, but failed,
at convincing Leo to stay home.

I'd waited until today,
while prepping the store to open,
before I approached Kit.
I hadn't trusted myself
to not scream at him too,
even if it wasn't his fault
and I was relieved
he hadn't taken part.

"Come into the back office
for a minute, Kit," I said,
"I want to talk with you."

Kit dragged behind me,
head down, struggling
to control his quivering lips.

He'd barely closed the door
before he began confessing.

"I don't think it's fair
that I be blamed for this.

Leo doesn't do anything
but what *he* wants to do.
I know I'm older,
but this idea that I can stop him,
or control him or guide him
is bullshit and you all know it.
Blaming me is just
finding someone to
blame other than yourselves."

"No one's blaming you," I half-lied.

"But you are! It's what you were going
to yell at me about as soon as I came in here.
I just beat you to it! I can *feel* how mad everyone
is at me and it's not fair. I didn't do *any* of it."

"Did you not know what he was planning?"

"I knew he was going to steal booze from
Great Giant but that was it."

I crossed my arms sternly but kept my tone even.
"How?"

"We've done it before. But after the last time,
I refused to do it again because Leo gets
unhinged. He's always doing more
and more. Nothing is ever fun enough for him."

"Why didn't you tell James or me?
We would have reeled him in."

"Oh, right! No one ever reels Leo in!
And to tell anyone meant I had to
confess my part and y'all are always
harder on me than him because
I'm older."

I realized then how true
that really was and it
wasn't fair.

I opened my arms
beckoning for him to
hug me.

Kit looked surprised
but came to me quickly
like he used to when he
was a young boy
when he'd stubbed his toe
or scraped his knee;
and just like then he let go
crying fully
and I held him until he
quieted down.

"It's not your fault,"
I said as I squeezed him

back, "and I'm sorry
we've always blamed you
for something so far out of
your control. I'm proud
of you for not going with him.
You did good, Kit. You did good."

## 52

Tuesday my car arrived,
delivered to a vacant parking
space adjacent to Pizza Palace
with a handwritten note
tucked under the wiper blade.

*Returning your car to you
was the least I could do. I know
it's not much but I hope it
helps. Remember to take care
and that this too shall pass.
Darcy*

I crumbled the paper
torn between reading
this as encouragement
or a polite escape.

I wanted to go to her,
but what would I say?

Asking her to choose me
despite all of her objections,
gut feelings, were right?
I couldn't do that.
She'd always deserve
better than what I
could give her.

## 53

By Wednesday afternoon,
Leo was released.
By evening of the same day,
I'd ignored a handful of calls
from various friends and family,
but was inevitably forced
to talk to him when he
showed up at my door.
Identified through the keyhole,
I wrestled between
walking away or letting him in.
I settled on the latter,
already annoyed as I opened the door.
"I didn't think you were going to answer,"
Leo puffed angrily.
"As astute as ever," I drawled in reply.
"What's your problem?" Leo snapped,
"You're the one who's been MIA.
That's why I'm here too!
Why are you avoiding me,
rather than supporting me?"

I felt my face twitching,
an overwhelming disappointment
bubbling up from deep down
understanding that we'd made Leo
into this arrogant narcissistic asshole
with all our sheltering, spoiling sentimentality.
Was rehabilitation (if possible)
our responsibility now or
would redemption only be found
if Leo passed nature's educational course?
"Look," Leo pressed on, when didn't respond,
I know I fucked up but I'm young and if you're
gonna fuck up, now is the time. I just can't belive
your hot rich girlfriend was there, and not you,
that's all I'm–"
"You saw Darcy?" I asked.
"Yeah, she was sitting in the audience;
I saw her pass something to the lawyer."
"Why was she there?"
Leo raised his hands.
"I don't know anything,
but I think its hypocritical
to be dating *the man* rather
than fighting him."
"The man?"
"She's *rich* and not from
where we're from.
Her highrise keeps her
far away from our troubles
and she can't be bothered

With what's happening down here,
but she came to court and you didn't?
Man, that's some traitorous shit."
I snatched my brother by the collar
And pulled him close,
"Are you telling me,
that ransacking our *own* hood
was tied to some idea of
fucking over rich people?"
"No, that was just fun
that went too far," Leo sputtered.
I released him,
taking many steps back.
"Unbelievable," I spat,
"Are you so dense you can't see
how hurting *our* tenants at *our*
mini-mart is bad for everyone?"
Leo shrugged.
"I got carried away, but,
that's what insurance is for."
"Get out," I roared.
"That still doesn't excuse you
from not showing up for family!"
"OUT!" I bellowed furiously.
Leo finally yielded.
"Fine, I'll go, but really,
thank your girlfriend for me.
I wasn't supposed to say anything,
but every bill we had,
even the reform school,

(straight bull that I have to go)
was paid in full before we got there.
Your girl is the only
money bags we know;
it has to be her."
I pushed him out of my apartment,
slamming the door so hard
it rattled on its hinges;
too stunned to speak.

# 54

"I PROMISE YOU," MISSIE insisted,
   "we don't know where the anonymous
   funds came from, but I imagine
   you have an idea?"
   I hadn't told my parents my theory.
   I didn't want my mother to feel indebted,
   and I didn't want my father to feel emboldened.
   Was I protecting Darcy's integrity
   or my own pride?
   Would Darcy really do
   all of that for me?
   I had to know for sure.
   "I'll reach out to our lawyer,
   let him know to expect your call.
   If there's any answers to be had,
   that's where you'll find them."

# 55

—•—

"Anonymity must be respected,
  Mr. Bennet," our family lawyer insisted.

I chucked the dish rag at the wall,
watched it slink down until
it made a satisfying plunk
into the water.

"Please share what you can,"
I bit out, fighting to keep
my tone civil.

"Most of it you already know–"
"Please, if you don't mind," I insisted.
Our lawyer sighed but conceded.

"Shortly after reviewing
the initial charges,
I received a visit
from a person
inquiring about becoming an

advocate for Leo.
We discussed what would most likely
sway a judge to be more lenient,
which generally is showing a
plan of action for correcting
the behavior and forcing
the minor to be accountable for their crime.
They then provided me with a check
to use at my leisure in conjunction
with whatever the family preferred.
The rest of the funds were to go
into a trust for the family
to use for repairs and reparations."

"I see," I murmured.
There was no doubt,
nor should there have been.
All of this was because of Darcy.
Empathy was always a choice,
never an act of god.
I knew that,
just my ego had driven me to
be *sure*.

I guess I needed to know exactly
how much I'd misjudged her.

I felt it all,
guilt,
regret,

stupidity,

irony,

and most potent

the realization that even if I

wanted to make this right

I didn't know how.

It was probably too little, too late,

but I had to try one more time.

## 56

I LET A FEW more days pass.

Marinated in the past,

while stewing in regret

as I tried to figure out my next move.

Calling felt too impersonal,

going to see her felt too intense,

but doing nothing felt insanely stupid.

I felt frozen

and panicked–

this was likely my last chance

to get it *right*.

*Maybe I didn't deserve to get it right,*

an insecure voice whispered in my head.

I'd taken a couple shifts,

Leo was going away soon to school,

and his face was such a sore spot

in the mini-mart that he couldn't work

at Pizza Palace even if we wanted him to.

Missie had plans to interview local kids,

but there just hadn't been time yet.

I didn't mind; the familiarity of the work

was soothing and distracting.

I was a dustinator-covered coward,

stuck in an indecision of my own making.

I didn't hear the customer approaching

until someone began rapid-fire-ringing

the counter bell for service.

**57**

—·—

*BIANCA.*

James saw her a split second after me
and his ecstatic energy blasted
through the pizza parlor.
He didn't speak,
he took action.
Hopping over the counter,
James swept her into his arms,
kissing her without any hesitation,
as if this might be his only chance
to express everything he'd been holding in.
Bianca melted right into him,
as if she'd been waiting, hoping,
for this moment too.
As they embraced, everything vanished.
It was just them;
no mini-mart, no differences, no past quarrels,
just two people who cared for each other
more than any doubts or fears
that'd once patrolled their minds.
I wanted to be that brave,

but–how could you be sure?
James broke the kiss,
spinning Bianca in a circle
as she giggled, cheeks flushed
from their kiss.
"Hi," James said, finally
setting Bianca down.
Bianca laughed,
rising up on her toes to
kiss him once again.
Our four mid-afternoon regulars hooted.
James whispered something to Bianca,
racing to the back of the store.
Clearly he was taking the day;
and I was elated for him.
Had Darcy done this too?
Sent Bianca back to right
the wrong of influencing her friend?
"You know, Elijah," Bianca said,
approaching the counter, "a little
romantic gesture of your own
wouldn't hurt."
"No?"
"It's never too late to tell someone
how you really feel," she said.
"You just have to be
brave enough to speak."
I nodded.
Bianca reached across the counter
squeezing my hand.

*"Go get your girl,"* Bianca encouraged.

# 58

I MADE IT TO Darcy's by 9:48 PM that night.
No plan but plenty of feelings,
desperately needing to be said.
She answered on the third ring.
"Elijah! How are you?"

Darcy sounded happy
which made me nervous
as if dumping these feelings
on her might shift her mood
but I was seeing this through,
I had to know for sure.

"Can we talk?" I asked
before I lost my nerve.
"Of course, what's up?"
"Good–I'll be up in a minute."
"Wait, you're here?"
"Yeah, see you soon?" I asked.
Darcy sounded surprised
but agreed and I promptly

hung up before I lost
all my newly found nerve.

# 59

DARCY ANSWERED THE DOOR
  on the second knock;
  as soon as our eyes met
  I knew she'd forever
  be the only one.
  "Don't say anything,
  not yet," I pleaded.

  Darcy nodded and
  I let myself come undone,
  the words flowing
  from my heart in a way
  I'd never allowed before.

  "I have to get this out
  before I lose my nerve," I continued
  "because I've been an
  ass and I know it.
  I don't deserve,
  god, what would this be now,
  a third or fourth chance?

Doesn't matter, the point is
I was wrong,
so wrong,
and if I'm too late
then I accept that but
I have to at least let you know
I love you more than
anyone I've ever loved
or will *ever love* and I need
you to know that
and if there's any part of you
still willing to give us a chance
I hope you will but just know
I'm an ass and I'll unintentionally
muck things up,
but I'll never deny loving you
or wanting you again."

Darcy came towards me then
sensing I'd gotten everything
out and took my left hand in hers,
bringing it to her cheek before
brushing a feather soft kiss
across my knuckles.

"Well then," she said
with a smile, "I
guess it's a good
thing I never stopped
loving you either."

I took her into my arms
hovering above her lips
just a moment,
taking her in
soaking up this
wild free range of
emotions surging through me
and then I let go
and kissed her they
way I should always
have been.

— . —

# EPILOGUE

IT'S NO SURPRISE THAT everything worked out,
well almost everything.

Leo is still Leo but,
he was young and
we were holding out hope
that reform school would reform him.
We were making progress
restoring morale and faith
within the community.
No one seemed to fully distrust us,
I suppose our forthright approach
to fixing, repairing, reimbursing
fostered a lot of good will,
but people were weary of Mario and Kit,
as if they couldn't help
but look at them and wonder
if one bad apple had in fact ruined the bunch.

Missie and Monte were doing just fine,
their joint effort and focus

it took to get sort out all the chaos
Leo had created actually had made them closer,
stronger in a way.
I believe my dad recognized his
flippant carefree behavior
had pathed the way for Leo to
be so *Leo*.
I'm sure those regrets
were coming into focus now.

Bianca and James
were a full blown couple now,
so much so that against
all practical advice from
me (or Darcy) they'd
moved in together.
We let it be though,
realizing we'd already
trifled in their relationship
more than we should have;
the ultimate lesson being:
a heart only beats for itself.

And Darcy and I,
did we get our happily ever after,
did our truce last longer than
a steamy fortnight,
did we successfully unlock
the enemies to friends to lovers
trifecta trope?

Of course we did!
What good is a romance story
without a happy ending?

# ACKNOWLEDGEMENTS

It's never easy to finish a project and it seems the longer I write the harder it becomes. You'd think it'd be the other way around, right? Apparently, not for me. This project was especially scary but as always I'm fortunate to have a handful of close friends and family cheering me on to write that weird idea and always ready to read my *very* rough drafts. Extra special thanks to my husband Nicholas, my son Lincoln, my ride or die pup Stark, my writing besties Jean Davis and Yong Takahashi and all the beautiful souls who let me borrow their pens at the Holland Writers' Group when I inevitably forget mine. I would not be the writer I am today without all the thought encouragment and gentle feedback I've been given. Thank you!

# About the Author

**Vera West** fell into a torrid love affair with creative writing in college and since then has written many novels and poetry collections examining the nature of love, redemption, cultural identity, social issues and the afterlife.